And they all lived happily ever after.

They lived happily ever after because . . .

the soggy knight fell in love with the clever Princess.

The knight fell in love with the Princess because . . .

She poured a big bowl of lemonade on top of his head.

She poured a bowl of lemonade on top of his head because . . .

the knight's curly red beard was on fire.

His curly red beard was on fire because . . .

he had been tickling a great green dragon.

the dragon would not stop crying.

The dragon would not stop crying because...

one hundred bunny rabbits had hopped into his cave and frightened him.

One hundred bunny rabbits had hopped into the dragon's cave because . . .

they were trying to escape an enormous
tomato rolling down the hill.

An enormous tomato was rolling down the hill because . . .

it had been hit by a flying teacup.

a hungry giant was throwing a temper tantrum.

The giant was throwing a tantrum because . . .

The cook did not make lemon cheesecake for dessert because...

there were no lemons

left at the market.

And there were no lemons

left at the market because...

once upon a time a clever princess

decided to make a big bowl of lemonade.

To Laurie Skiba
—D.L.
To Denise for her famous
flat lemon cake
—R.E.

ISBN-13: 978-0-439-64012-1
ISBN-10: 0-439-64012-1

Arthur A. Levine Books hardcover edition published by Arthur A. Levine Books, an imprint of Scholastic Inc., January 2007

12 11 10 9 8 7 6 5 4 3 2   8 9 10 11 12 13/0

Printed in the U.S.A.   08

First paperback printing, May 2008 · Book design by Elizabeth B. Parisi · Hand-lettering by Georgia Deaver

THE

Story by David LaRochelle

SCHOLASTIC INC.

END

Illustrations by Richard Egielski

New York Toronto London Auckland Sydney
Mexico City New Delhi Hong Kong Buenos Aires